MARRY ME

Dan Rhodes

Marry Me

Europa
editions

Europa Editions
214 West 29th Street
New York, N.Y. 10001
www.europaeditions.com
info@europaeditions.com

Copyright © 2013 by Dan Rhodes
Published by arrangement with Canongate Books Ltd,
14 High Street, Edinburgh EH1 1TE
First Publication 2014 by Europa Editions

Library of Congress Cataloging in Publication Data is available
ISBN 978-1-60945-181-3

Rhodes, Dan
Marry Me

Book design by Emanuele Ragnisco
www.mekkanografici.com

Cover photo © Sisoje/iStock

Prepress by Grafica Punto Print – Rome

Printed in the USA

For wife-features, of course

Marriage is the only legal contract which abrogates
as between the parties all the laws that safeguard
the particular relation to which it refers.
—GEORGE BERNARD SHAW

Author's note:
I have no idea what this means, but I'm sure it's very wise

Contents

MARRY ME

Ex

From the moment I met her, my girlfriend wouldn't stop talking about her ex. Time and again she told me about the charming things he would say and do, and I came to learn every detail of the sun-drenched and culturally enlightening holidays they had taken together. She often told me how safe she had felt when she was by his side, and that they had experienced an indescribable quality of closeness during sex. Whenever I surprised her with a present she would be quick to tell me that his choice of gift had always been perfect, as if he could see inside her mind. 'It wasn't to be,' she would sigh, 'but I make do.'

Eventually, she agreed to marry me. On our wedding night, as she lay naked in my arms, she said, 'It's funny—if things had turned out just a little bit different, it would have been him I'd just done that with, not you.'

TERMS AND CONDITIONS

To say my fiancée was pregnant on our wedding day would be an understatement. She was enormous, and when she reached the altar she let out a howl, clutched her belly and lowered herself to the floor, puffing and panting as she struggled to find a comfortable position for delivery. My mother rushed to her side, reached under her wedding dress and blocked the baby's exit with her hands.

'Hurry up,' she shouted at the vicar. 'No grandchild of mine is being born out of wedlock.'

The vicar and I did our best to keep things moving along, but we weren't helped by my bride's lack of cooperation. Instead of vows, all we heard were grunts, wails and language quite inappropriate for the surroundings. Eventually we managed to get her to agree to the terms and conditions, and after a struggle I was able to get the ring on her finger.

At last my mother was able to withdraw her hands and return to her pew. My bride carried on with her wailing, cursing and sweating. There was quite a lot of gunk by this point, and like everybody else I didn't know quite what to say or where to look.

SOULS

My wife had always told me that whenever we made love she had seen it as not so much a sexual thing, more a union of souls.

'But I thought you meant that in a good way.'

'I didn't mean it in a bad way,' she said. 'But let's face it, there was a pretty big hint in there; and to be honest, the "souls" thing has started wearing *really* thin.'

I asked her whether this meant that she was giving up on me.

'No,' she said, 'I'm not giving up on you. I'm just asking you to do it better from now on. A lot better.'

ALIBI

My wife was arrested for a crime she didn't commit. While she was in custody, the police sent their toughest detective around to question me about her movements. 'Is it true that you spent the evening of Tuesday the seventeenth gazing adoringly at the suspect, and gently stroking her face?' he asked.

I told him it was.

'But it makes no sense,' he said, scratching his chin. 'She's so plain. Why would you do such a thing?'

'She may not be a beauty queen,' I said, 'but I love her with all my heart, and to me she's the prettiest girl in the world.'

'You don't expect me to believe that?'

'No,' I sighed, 'I don't suppose I do. But it's true.'

HER OLD SELF

I arrived at the hospital to find my girlfriend slipping away. To bring her comfort in her final hours, I asked her to marry me. She accepted, and surrounded by our immediate family and closest friends we held a ceremony where she lay. Her voice was so halting that there were moments when I wondered whether she would even make it to the end of the vows.

As soon as the ring was on her finger she began to recover, and within minutes she was sitting up. I couldn't believe what I was seeing; I would never have married her if I'd thought for a moment that she was going to live. 'I'm off to the pub to celebrate,' I said, desperate to get away.

'You're doing no such thing,' she snapped.

'You still haven't put up the blind in the spare room. And have you called that man about unblocking the drain in the back yard? And it's your turn to clean the windows—inside and out this time. And it's bin day tomorrow, if you could remember to put them out for once in your life . . .' It was relentless. I couldn't understand why everybody else was so happy to see her back to her old self. 'And let's not forget that there's the small matter of the consummation to be dealt with,' she said.

The others discreetly withdrew, and we were left alone.

'Don't just stand there,' she barked. 'Get on with it.'

PREDICTABLE

Starlight told me she had decided to call time on our marriage. When I asked her why, she said I had become too predictable. I begged her to reconsider. 'I don't know what I would do without you,' I sobbed.

She shook her head in exasperation. 'I *knew* you were going to say that.'

VEIL

Determined that whoever she married would love her for who she was, regardless of what she looked like, Amethyst refused to let her suitors see her face. Throughout our courtship she went out of her way to make sure I had no idea what lay behind the impenetrable layers of scarves, balaclavas and dark glasses that she always wore. I was captivated by her lively conversation, though, and before long I knew for sure that she was the girl for me. I was over the moon when she agreed to be my wife, and as she walked down the aisle I had no idea what I was going to see when she lifted her veil. I had a strong feeling she would be either heart-stoppingly beautiful or stomach-churningly gruesome, but I knew I would love her just the same either way. When the moment came, and I saw her face for the first time, I couldn't believe my eyes.

She was reasonably pretty. Not plain, but certainly nothing special. I couldn't quite work out why she had gone to all that trouble.

STICK

I opened the front door to find my ex-wife standing there, looking even lovelier than I remembered. 'You've come back,' I cried, overcome with joy.

'God, no,' she said. 'You've completely got the wrong end of the stick. The shops are shut, and my new husband needs some WD-40. You keep some under the sink, don't you?' Hunched in defeat, I went to the kitchen to fetch it. She followed, and stood watching as I rummaged for the can. 'He's working on his motorbike,' she explained. 'With his top off.'

CHALLENGES

Oleander told me that after careful consideration she had decided to move on to fresh challenges. 'This has not been an easy decision to make,' she said, 'but I feel the time is right.' She told me she felt privileged to have had such a rewarding experience as our marriage, and that her stint as my wife had helped her to develop a valuable set of skills. She thanked me for the opportunities I had offered her, wished me all the best for the future, and told me she was prepared to remain in my life for one calendar month, during which she would do everything she could to make my transition back to single status as smooth as possible.

NEWS

As our wedding day approached, I became increasingly unsure about the idea of spending the rest of my life with my fiancée. I started to think quite seriously about calling everything off. As I was explaining this to my friend Demetrio, news came through that she had been horribly mauled by an escaped tiger. I rushed to the hospital and found her lying there, eyes peeping through a gap in her bandages. I knew then that I had to tell her about my misgivings.

She accused me of jilting her because she had lost her looks. Luckily, I had foreseen this possibility, and brought Demetrio along to back me up. His English isn't great, but with a few disjointed phrases and an elaborate mime he was able to verify that my doubts had already been in place. He has a trustworthy expression, and she was able to accept that my love just wasn't strong enough for us to enter into marriage. After she'd had a little cry, I reassured her that we could still be friends.

'But what about the tiger?' she asked. She had always been so fond of animals. 'They didn't kill it, did they?' Her eyes widened with concern. 'Tell me they didn't kill it.'

They had killed it, though—they'd shot it through the face with a giant gun. Demetrio provided her with a speculative re-enactment of its final moments, and she fell into a fresh wave of sobs. Dealing with that kind of thing was no longer my responsibility, and after weighing up my options I decided to leave her to it.

JUDGE

Hoping to save our marriage, I wouldn't agree to my wife's request for a divorce. We ended up in front of a judge, who took one look at her and one look at me, and started laughing. 'Do you seriously think I'm going to make *her* stay married to *you*?'

My now-ex-wife gave me one of her *I told you so* looks, and as usual I had no choice but to concede that she had been right all along.

THE FUNNY SIDE

'You always try to see the funny side of a situation, don't you?' said my wife. I nodded enthusiastically, wondering what she was going to tell me. 'Here's a situation for you,' she said. 'I'm leaving.'

No matter how hard I looked, I couldn't see a funny side. I asked her to help me find the humour.

'Do you remember that time you told me I was way out of your league, and how you were worried that one day I would find somebody a lot more handsome than you, and much, much better in bed? Well, now I have. That's funny, isn't it?'

I stood frozen.

'Couldn't you at least *pretend* to find it

amusing?' she snapped, clearly running out of patience.

I had hoped never to disappoint her, and using all that remained of my strength I forced my lips into a grin. A sob escaped me, and I did my best to turn it into a chuckle.

'That's better,' she said, picking up her holdall. 'I don't feel so bad now.' As she walked down the garden path and out of my life, I could see my smiling face reflected in her tight, black PVC mini skirt.

I was delighted when my scientist girlfriend agreed to become my fiancée. 'This is the happiest moment of my life,' I said.

'Mine, too,' she replied. 'I'm experiencing an unprecedented rush of dopamine and norepinephrine. Of course the production of these particular neurotransmitters will decrease over time, but I have a pretty good feeling that our vasopressin levels will remain adequate, and we'll be fine for the long haul. But never mind all that,' she said, taking off her goggles and unbuttoning her lab coat. 'What do you say we release a bit of the old oxytocin?'

When I knew for sure that I wasn't going to get better, and that time was running out, I summoned all my inner strength and tearfully told my wife that she wasn't to feel bad about moving on. 'You're a young, attractive woman with so much ahead of you,' I said. 'I don't want you growing old alone. When you feel ready to let somebody else into your life, then you should—with my blessing.'

'It's so good of you to say so,' she said, squeezing my hand. 'And your timing's just perfect—I met this *gorgeous* man on the way here. He gave me his number, but I wasn't sure about calling him because of all this business.' She indicated my outstretched body, tubes running in and out of it at various points. 'But

41

now I know we have your blessing . . . She reached into her bag and found her phone. 'He's a real catch—he'll be snapped up by another girl if I drag my heels.'

I was dismayed that she had found a replacement quite so quickly, and my face must have betrayed my feelings.

'Oh, don't worry,' she said. 'I'll tell him right from the start that there's no way he'll be getting lucky until after the funeral.' She dialled his number, and as she waited for a reply she carried on. 'Well, maybe not after the funeral itself, but I won't let him do a thing until you're *completely* dead.'

CHILDREN

I begged my wife to stay. 'Please,' I said. 'For the children's sake.'

'But we don't have any children.'

'I know. But I had always hoped that one day . . .'

MISTAKES

On our honeymoon my wife lay beside me, writing a letter to her best friend. When she had finished, she asked me to check it over. I was glad to help, so I carefully read it through. Her handwriting is very neat, and her spelling and grammar are pretty good, but there were one or two minor glitches for me to point out. 'See here?' I said. 'You've written "the most biggest mistake I have ever made"—but it should just be "the biggest mistake I have ever made." And this bit, where you've put "it feels like a life sentance," that should be "sentence".' I'd only caught one more error. 'Where you've written "I dont know what I did to deserve this," you need an apostrophe in "don't".' I explained that it was a contraction,

45

and that it was the job of the apostrophe to take the place of the missing letter. She looked very serious, nodding just a little as she took it all in.

HUNGRY

My bride didn't turn up at the church. The reception was cancelled, and I had no idea what to do with the cake. As I carried it through the streets I saw some peckish-looking tramps and offered it to them, but they told me they didn't like marzipan. I said I wouldn't be offended if they were to pick it off, but they told me very politely that just knowing it had had marzipan on it would make them feel sick.

The idea of cutting into it and eating it on my own made me so sad that I knew I couldn't do it. With trembling hands, I called my ex-fiancée. 'Darling,' I said, 'what should I do with the cake?'

'I'm not your darling any more,' she said. 'I left you, remember?'

'Oh yes. Sorry. But what should I do with it?'

She sighed, and called out to someone. 'Are you hungry?'

I could hear a man's voice. 'Only for you,' it said.

She giggled. 'Just feed it to the ducks,' she told me, and hung up.

I supposed that was as good an idea as any. I carried it to the pond in the park, but even the ducks weren't interested. Piece by piece I threw it in, watching each one float, ignored, on the surface before becoming waterlogged and sinking into the silt.

PROMISE

I told Aveline I was leaving. She gave me one of her looks, and said, 'My memory of the wedding is that you promised to love me forever, no matter what.'

'Oh, bloody hell,' I said. 'I'd forgotten about that.' Under the circumstances there wasn't much I could do but carry on being married to her. It's not worked out too badly. On balance, I'm quite glad we've stayed together.

Her Way

One cloudless night, on a starlit beach, I decided that the moment had come. I lowered myself to one knee, and asked Ammonite if she would do me the honour of being my bride. Her sweet face lit up. 'Yes,' she said. 'Yes, I will.' Overjoyed, I took her in my arms and tenderly kissed her.

When we parted, I noticed that the gentle expression I had grown to love had changed to one I hadn't seen on her before: cold fury. 'Right,' she snarled. 'The last wedding we went to had a string quartet, so we're going to need at least a *quin*tet. And I'm not letting anyone bring children; I don't want shrieking brats running around. I'm having a Bentley, not a Rolls, and none of the guests are to wear coral, salmon or peach—I'm adamant about that . . .'

Hours later, as the sun came up, she was still going. '. . . Sandra from work will expect to be at the church, but she's only coming to the disco. And don't go thinking that friend of yours with the stupid hair is being invited— I've never liked him, and I'm not going to have him *or* his hair in the photos.' With no end in sight, I told myself that above all it was going to be Ammonite's day, and the best thing would be to let her have her way.

'Yes, dear,' I said, in the rare moments when she paused to draw breath. 'Of course, dear.'

FUSS

In the run up to our wedding day, my fiancée told me to be quiet. 'Can't you change the subject?' she snapped. 'All I've been hearing lately is "I love you so much," and "We have such a wonderful future ahead of us," and "I can't believe I'm going to marry the girl of my dreams".' She closed her eyes and shook her head. 'It's a legal procedure; let's just get through it with the minimum of fuss.'

Silver explained that while she loved me very much as a friend, she couldn't see us settling down together. She had anticipated my distress, and was quick to comfort me. 'Don't worry,' she said. 'You won't have to be alone.' She reached into her bag and brought out a brochure full of pictures of marriageminded Russian women. Leafing through it, she pointed at the ones she thought I would like, reading out their names, ages, heights and interests.

'But what if I don't want a Russian bride?' I asked.

'Don't be silly,' she said. 'It'll help you get over me. And besides, I've always thought you would make a wonderful husband for some lucky girl.' One Russian in particular had caught her eye. 'Look,' she said, 'she's got such lovely hair. You two will be *so* happy together.'

I told her I was going to spend every moment of the rest of my life wishing she hadn't left me, and that would hardly be fair on the Russian.

'Listen,' she said. 'I'm moving on, and it would really help me to know that you've moved on too.' She gave me a pleading look. 'So what do you say? Will you write to her?'

Silver knew I would do anything for her, and there was nothing I could do but nod. She jumped up and down, squealing with delight. 'Can I be a bridesmaid?' she asked. 'Oh, can I? It's only fair—you two would never have met if it hadn't been for me.'

I agreed to let her be a bridesmaid. Veruschka is due to arrive any day now. I'll try as hard as I can to love her, for Silver's sake.

HAT

My mother told me that the time had come for my girlfriend and I to legitimise our sex life. She had a point, so a few days later I found myself down on one knee in a romantic location. Unfortunately, I was rejected. My girlfriend told me she just wasn't able to see us growing old together, that I had never been quite as good in bed as she had hoped, and that under the circumstances it would be best not to drag things out any longer.

When I broke the news to my mother, she was furious. She had already bought a massive hat. She took it out of its box, put it on her head and pointed at it. 'What am I supposed to do with this fucking thing now?' she bellowed.

RING

My girlfriend had been a real nuisance, and even though she was incredibly good-looking I had been thinking quite seriously about splitting up with her. Since her lobotomy, though, things have improved, and I'm starting to see a way forward for us as a couple. These days I can leave coins and cigarettes lying around without having to worry about her stealing them, and she's even started smiling, in a vacant sort of way. None of my friends had liked her very much, but they're starting to change their opinions. 'If you're still thinking about packing her in,' they say, looking her up and down with hunger in their eyes, 'I'd be glad to take her off your hands.' A while ago I'd have relinquished her on the spot, but not any more. I'm even thinking about putting a ring on her finger, to mark her as mine. She won't notice, but it'll still count.

FRIENDS

My wife told me she was leaving, and I was heartbroken. Clutching at straws, I asked her if we could still be friends.

'Let's be realistic,' she said. 'I've been through this so many times, and take it from me—the *friends* thing never really works.'

'So I'll never see you again?' I sobbed.

'No,' she said, sympathetically patting my arm, 'I'm afraid not. But if it's any consolation, you'll be hearing from my solicitor.'

LOOKS

I came to the realisation that I would love my girlfriend just the same even if she lost her looks. 'This means I'm definitely ready for us to get married,' I said.

She looked thoughtful. 'If you were to lose your looks,' she said 'I think I would love you quite a lot less.'

I was worried. 'Does this mean you won't marry me?'

'No, I might as well. It's a gamble, but I've always had a reckless streak.'

My wife had been unemployed for ages, so I was delighted when she applied for work as a classical composer. Neither of us knew much about that kind of thing, but they must have been impressed by her enthusiasm because she got the job. They sent her on a training course, and a few weeks later I went along to the premiere of her first symphony.

I was struck by how professional it sounded, and enjoyed a lot of the tunes. When it was over, I listened to the people sitting next to me as they discussed their interpretations of the piece. They agreed that the first movement had been as bleak and brave a portrayal of a failing marriage as they had ever heard; the second, they said, had been about escaping the emptiness of this marriage by embarking upon a passionate affair with a handsome bassoonist; and the consensus was that the third had dealt with the final escape, leaving the grinding tedium behind to begin an exciting new life.

I tracked her down backstage. 'You didn't mean any of that, did you?' I asked.

She nodded. 'Every note. I'm sorry you had to find out this way, but at least it's out in the open now.' She gave my shoulder a sympathetic squeeze, told me her brother would be round for her things, then left to begin her first world tour.

FREUD

I never seemed to meet the kind of girl I would like to settle down with, but after reading Sigmund Freud I realised where I had been going wrong. I took out a lonely hearts ad that said: *Do you resemble this woman? If so, I would be interested in marriage.* Underneath was a photograph of my mother. Unfortunately, it didn't work quite as well as I'd hoped. I only received one reply, and although she seemed quite promising on paper, I got to the rendezvous to find I'd been corresponding with my sister.

I don't know what she was thinking. If anything she takes after our father's side of the family.

LEMMINGS

My bride was determined to be the most beautiful girl at her wedding, and had gone out of her way to look her best for the big day. As we danced cheek to cheek at the reception, she whispered, 'Have you seen the way the men have been looking at me? They can't believe what they're seeing. There are going to be some suicides tonight, I can tell you.'

I wasn't so sure. I thought she was wearing too much make-up, and her hair looked really stiff. Quite a lot of the other girls looked better than her, but I decided that under the circumstances it would be best to keep my opinions to myself. 'They'll be jumping off the roof like lemmings,' I said.

POTS AND PANS

My wife told me that while she loved me very much, she was no longer in love with me. 'I'll be staying here, and keeping all the pots and pans,' she continued, 'so your new place is going to need a little stocking up.' She pulled out a catalogue and started pointing to various items of kitchenware, praising their style and making claims about their versatility and longevity. 'How would you feel if I was to say that *you* could own some of these extraordinary pieces?' she asked.

Dazed, I found myself signing up to buy three saucepans, a frying pan and an oven dish, as well as a number of associated accessories.

'You're my first customer,' she said, sealing the deal with a firm handshake. 'I would give

you a discount because I know you, but it's
early days and I'm sure you'll understand that
I've got to keep a firm grip on my finances now
I'm a single gal.'

My wife handed me an envelope, and I excitedly tore it open to find a greetings card with a picture of some kittens on it. I looked inside, and in her neatest handwriting she had written: *Thank you so much for putting up with me through my lesbian phase.*

'What lesbian phase?' I asked.

'Oh,' she said, looking surprised, 'it's been going on for about two years. I thought it was obvious: the short hair; the dungarees; the way I wouldn't let you touch me.'

I was stupefied, but the more I thought about it, the more it made sense. I couldn't believe I hadn't read the signals.

'But never mind all that,' she said, reaching

up to ruffle my hair. 'I'm back to normal now. I'll go and put on loads of make-up, and we can pretend it never happened.'

CHURCH

My fiancée had never been even slightly religious, but she was determined to have a traditional wedding. 'There's just something nice about churches,' she said. 'They're really old, and stuff like that.' After looking at quite a few, she chose her favourite, and we went along to talk through the arrangements. All the time, I could see she was stifling giggles, and as soon as we were outside she got on the phone to her sister and told her all about it. 'There was this man in a dress,' she guffawed, 'and he kept going on and on about God.'

When she'd hung up, I asked if she would rather look for a more secular venue, but she was adamant that we stick to her original plan. 'It's so weddingy in there, with all those colourful windows and the candles and that weird-sounding piano.' Then she thought of something. 'Wait here,' she said. 'I'm going back to ask that man to pray for sunshine. That kind of thing's probably not real, but it's worth a try because you never know.'

COLD

A week before our wedding day, my fiancée suggested I go into suspended animation and leave all the lastminute preparations to her. At first I wasn't sure about the idea, but she soon convinced me that it would be best for both of us if I was to take something of a back seat. She took me to the local cryogenic freezing centre, and told me she would thaw me out on the morning of the big day. She kissed me good-bye, and shut the door to the chamber.

When I unfroze, there was no one there to meet me. I walked over to her place to see how things were getting along. She saw me coming up the path, and called out, 'Look, everyone, it's the Iceman.' As I got closer, I noticed she looked a bit different, in a way I couldn't quite put my finger on. A tall, handsome man I had never seen before came out of the house, followed by a group of children, and they all started pointing at me and laughing.

She explained that she'd had cold feet, and hadn't been able to resist setting the timer for fifteen years. Then she stopped laughing, and her face turned to stone. She told me she hardly remembered me, and that it was time I left. She said I was trespassing, and that she would be well within her rights to call the police.

New Direction

As our wedding day approached, my fiancée became increasingly excited about the new direction our lives were taking. 'Just think of all the pathetic stuff we'll be able to do,' she said. 'We can watch cookery shows together, and talk about curtains, and have really boring friends. And we can go to bed early—not to have sex, just to fall asleep.' She sighed. 'It's what I've always wanted.'

It was what I had always wanted, too. I almost felt ready to start right then, by delivering an impenetrable monologue on the subject of aspect ratios, or droning on and on about my plans to upgrade the lawnmower, but I took a deep breath and stopped myself. It didn't seem right. I knew I had to be patient; some things would just have to wait until we were married.

Data

At our wedding rehearsal dinner, I stood up and brought the room to a hush with a tap of my glass. I told our guests that the moment I met Arnemetia I had known that I was ready to spend the rest of my life with her. As one, everybody sighed, and the bride-to-be wiped a tear of joy from her eye. I went on to explain that my love for her was so strong that I had immediately started gathering data about her. At this point I started projecting some of my findings on to a big screen. There was a line graph depicting the changing length of her hair over time; a series of diagrams showing the colours she had favoured in her wardrobe month by month; and an elaborate bubble chart documenting the complexity of her moods. She'd had no idea that I'd been collecting this information, but unfortunately she didn't appear to be delighted by the surprise.

'I can't work out if that's romantic or creepy,' she said. She asked our friends and family to help her decide, and with a show of hands they gave their opinions. Unfortunately, eighty-four per cent of them thought it was creepy, while a disappointing sixteen per cent thought it romantic. A further poll revealed that a comparable majority would fully understand were the wedding not to proceed.

Awkward

Several years into our engagement, I took my fiancée's hand and told her that the time had finally come for us to pin down a wedding date.

'This is awkward,' she said. 'I was *really* drunk when I agreed to all that, and sober there's just no way.'

Perfect

We spent every penny we could get our hands on making sure our wedding was perfect. With a lot of hard work we got it exactly right; every detail was in place for the happiest day of our lives.

When we returned from our honeymoon we found we weren't able to stay on top of the bills, and we soon lost our home. It was all worth it, though, and we don't regret a thing.

Now, years later, as we huddle together for warmth under whichever bridge happens to feel the safest, we reminisce about our special day.

'Wasn't it wonderful?' says my wife, breaking off from a conversation about how we wish we had some boric acid to keep the cockroaches at bay. 'I'll never forget the place settings. The calligraphy was exquisite.'

'I know,' I say, 'and what about the bridesmaids' corsages? To think the florist told us we'd be hard pressed to source that shade of orchid.'

We throw our heads back in laughter.

'And do you remember Uncle Desmond?' she chuckles, her eyes bright with the memory. I chuckle, too. At the reception Uncle Desmond had done an amusing dance with his arms outstretched, as though he were an aeroplane, or a bird or something.

Lemon

Lily of the Valley told me that, as an educated person, I must have known there was a one in three chance that a married couple of our demographic background would end up separating. 'So, don't start acting like this is completely unexpected,' she said. A car horn sounded outside, and I didn't see what I could do but stand there like a lemon as she picked up her holdall and walked out of my life.

ALONE

My wife died, and as I tended to my broken heart I was surprised by how many girls came around to offer their condolences. Without exception they steered the conversation in the same direction, telling me that while they were very sorry that she had slipped away, they had always thought I could have done better. It was so relentless that before long I began to wonder whether they had a point, and that I ought to aim quite a lot higher for my next marriage. Their visits continued, and eventually I whittled them down to a shortlist of six. When decision time came, I lined them up and got ready to make my final choice. They all had longer legs, more lustrous hair and glossier lips than my first wife, and none of them wore glasses or had a slightly haphazard nose like she had. Even so, I realised that none of them could ever take her place. 'I'm sorry,' I said, 'but I miss her so much, and it just wouldn't be fair on anyone.'

'Come on, girls,' said the one with the most make-up on. 'Let's go. I always had a feeling there was something funny about him.' Clutching their tiny bags, they stormed off, leaving me alone at last.

Two

Some years into our marriage, my wife asked me why, when there were so many different kinds of sex to choose from, I had only ever done the same two.

Kindness

My wife told me she was adamant that our separation be amicable; that the last thing she wanted was for us to become one of those former couples who only had bad things to say about one another. These sentiments were so reasonable, and so eloquently expressed, that I found it impossible to disagree. Even so, I was unable to disguise my anguish. Until that moment I'd thought our marriage had been going really well.

She saw how upset I was, and with her customary kindness she set out to soothe me. 'Would it help you to see a picture of my new boyfriend?' she asked.

Without waiting for an answer, she reached into her bag and pulled out a photograph. He was incredibly handsome. Smiling roguishly in aviator shades, he was sitting at the wheel of a sports car, rolled-up sleeves revealing muscular arms.

'You can't see his eyes in this one, but my God . . .' As she saw the agony on my face, her dreamy expression changed to one of concern. 'You do understand, don't you?' She held the photograph beside my face, and kept looking from one to the other. 'It's a no-brainer, isn't it?'

CARBON

I asked my girlfriend to marry me, and she said yes. I couldn't afford a diamond, so instead I handed her a lump of charcoal. 'It's pure carbon,' I explained. 'Now, if we can just find a way to rearrange the atoms . . .'

She stared at the black lump in her palm, and I began to worry that ours was going to be the shortest engagement in history. She smiled. 'We'll put it under the mattress,' she said. 'Maybe we'll squash it into a diamond over time.'

It's been there ever since. We check up on it every once in a while, and it never looks any different. I think we would be a bit disappointed if it ever did.

ROMANTICO

When my wife returned from a holiday with her friends, I was impatient to look through her photos. I was dismayed to see that in most of them a tall, handsome man was by her side, and in quite a few they were holding hands and kissing. 'Who's he?' I asked.

She told me his name was Romantico, that they were very much in love, and that he was going to come and get her, to take her back to his country. 'I want you to think of it as a fresh start for all three of us,' she said. I tried to talk her out of it, but it was no use; all I could do was look on as she waited by the front door, her holdall by her feet. That was over six years ago, and she's still waiting.

As she stood there we arranged our divorce,

and after a while I met somebody new, and remarried. At first my new wife was unsettled by her predecessor's constant presence in our hallway, but over time she's become used to her. We find it handy to have her there in case a delivery arrives while we're out. Whenever the bell rings she'll open the door in delight, and cry 'Romantico, I knew you would come,' before realising that it isn't him, sobbing a little bit, then signing for whatever's arrived. Last time it was a food processor.

My wife had been married so many times before that she knew exactly what to expect on our special day. 'My favourite bit is always the vows and the rings and all that,' she said, 'but I never like it when they make you write in that big book. It's really boring, and the audience just sort of sits there.' She was right—as we signed the register, I could sense that the guests didn't quite know what to do with themselves. 'Hurry up,' she whispered. 'We're losing them.'

REVEALING

My wife feels desperately sorry for women who wear revealing clothes. Whenever we're out together and we pass a girl in a short skirt that offers an uninterrupted view of long, smooth legs, she'll tut, and mutter something like, 'It's such a pity—she's got no self-respect.' I completely agree with her; if I'm ever out on my own and happen to catch a glimpse of a young lady in a dress so tight that it clings to every contour of her supple body, showing in minute detail the luxuriant shape of her breasts and the outline of her pert behind, I am consumed by an overwhelming sadness. Sighing, I look away almost as quickly as I can.

CART

After living together for over five years, there wasn't much left for us to talk about, and sex-wise we were down to once a fortnight. I was spending more and more of my free time in the garden shed, sorting through my toolbox, and most evenings she would be round at her sister's, watching soap operas and complaining about me. There was no getting away from it—we needed to have a serious talk about our future.

After a long conversation, we agreed that the time had finally come for us to get married. As soon as we had made the decision, her eyes filled with a light that I hadn't seen for a long time. 'Everyone will be so happy for us,' she sighed. She rushed to the shop, and came back minutes later clutching a wedding magazine. She leafed through it, *ooh*ing and *aah*ing at the pictures. 'Look at these people,' she squealed, pointing. 'They're in a horse and cart.'

I supposed I could put up with going in a horse and cart.

My friends are all married to very attractive women, and my wife couldn't help but feel a little insecure about this. When we got home after a night out with them it all boiled over, and she started to make spiteful comments. I gave her a hug, and told her that while she may not be in their league, she still had an awful lot going for her.

'Really?' she said, glad of the reassurance.

'Really.' I reached for a pen and a pad of paper, and together we set out to compile a list of her attributes. By daybreak, all we had written was that she had almost kicked her heroin habit, and that her new hairstyle might start suiting her once it had had a chance to grow out a bit.

Per Cent

My wife started introducing me to people as 'My current husband'.

'Darling,' I said, smiling at her choice of words, 'what's all this "current" business? People will think you're looking to move on.'

'I hadn't thought about that,' she said. 'I suppose they would—but then again, they wouldn't be a hundred per cent wrong.'

I felt my balance go. 'How many per cent wrong would they be?'

She looked serious for a while and bit her lip, then her expression relaxed. 'Zero per cent,' she said.

Whenever we were invited to a wedding, my girlfriend would be fiercely critical of even the slightest display of extravagance. 'Remember what Goethe said,' she would whisper, at the first sign of ostentation. '*One should only celebrate a happy ending; celebrations at the outset exhaust the joy and energy needed to urge us forward and sustain us in the long struggle. And of all celebrations a wedding is the worst; no day should be kept more quietly and humbly.*' I was inclined to agree, so when she accepted my proposal I looked forward to a simple ceremony among our immediate family and very closest friends.

One thing led to another, and a year later I found myself in a white suit, riding a bejewelled ostrich across a castle drawbridge and into an enormous room packed with guests, plenty of whom neither of us particularly liked.

Shortly, an eighteen-horn fanfare heralded the arrival of my bride. She rode in on a white horse with what looked like an ice cream cone stuck to its head in an attempt to make it look like a unicorn.

'What would Goethe have made of all this, then?' I asked her, as we dismounted and prepared to exchange vows.

'Ah, who cares?' she said, glowing with delight.

FATE

When it comes to matters of romance, my fiancée is a firm believer in destiny. 'If fate has decreed that I end up married to you,' she'll sigh, 'then there's not much I can do about it, is there?'

DRESS

My wife's final wish was to be cremated in her wedding dress, and when she slipped away I tenderly prepared her body just as she had asked.

When I carried her into the funeral parlour, the undertaker took one look at her and shook his head. With impeccable politeness, he explained that even though the dress was very small, the black rubber it was made from would cause a terrible mess in the furnace, as well as sending an acrid aroma through the surrounding streets. 'I am afraid, sir,' he said, 'that there are rules about this kind of thing.' He saw the dismay on my face. 'Perhaps,' he suggested, 'madam had something in her wardrobe which was comparably whorish, but rather more likely to conform to council regulations?'

CHEER

My wife told me she had turned herself inside out trying to find a way ahead for us as a couple, but no matter how hard she looked she just couldn't see one. She knew in her heart that our marriage had run its course. I didn't know what to say, and just stood there looking really sad. In an attempt to cheer me up, she started tickling me. 'Tickle tickle tickle,' she said. It didn't work; I just carried on looking despondent. She tried again. 'Tickle tickle tickle.' I remained downcast. 'Wow,' she said. 'You're taking this even worse than I thought you would.'

Six months into our marriage, my wife told me she was leaving. 'It's not going to be easy for you,' she said, 'but there are plenty of positives you can take from the situation. Mainly, you should just be grateful that you had me at all— most men don't get near a girl like me their whole lives.' She handed me a photograph album containing page after page of pictures of herself in erotic poses, and explained that she had been compiling it over the preceding weeks, with the intention of helping to soften the blow of her departure. 'It's all very tasteful,' she said. 'There's no split beaver, or anything like that.'

I leafed through it, and there she was, draping her bikini-clad body across a motorcycle, pouting in high heels and lingerie on a mountaintop, and fondling her naked breasts under a waterfall. She told me I was welcome to show it to my friends and family, and brag to them about having had repeated sex with someone as hot as her. 'I did one for my last husband when I left him,' she said, 'and I know it really helped.'

The trouble is, she's nowhere near as attractive as she thinks she is; if anything she's a bit funnylooking, and the photographs amounted to something of a horror show. As she picked up her holdall and walked away, I didn't have the heart to tell her I had only ever loved her for her personality.

CORDIAL

Along with the traditional vows, my bride and I promised one another that we would always remain on cordial terms. As I gazed into her beautiful eyes and slipped the ring on her finger, it felt so wonderful to know that if things were to go wrong, even to the extent of a third party becoming involved, we would at least be civil about it.

When my ex-girlfriend called and suggested we meet up in her home town, I agreed straight away. It was wonderful to see her again; she was looking prettier than ever, and when she gave me a hug it felt just like the old days. After a little small talk, she took my arm and guided me towards a lavishly decorated open trailer, with a large and diverse group of dazedlooking men standing on it. 'I've invited all my former lovers here today,' she explained. 'Everyone in town has heard so much about you lot, and I thought it would be nice for them to get to see you; the carnival parade is the perfect opportunity. So,' she said, pointing at the float, 'on you get.'

I clambered up, then watched as she ushered several more ashen faced men on board

When, at last, we were all accounted for, she addressed us through a megaphone, instructing us to smile and wave at the people lining the streets. 'And here's the best part,' she continued, her amplified voice reverberating through the summer air. 'I've decided that it's time for me to settle down—and one of you boys is going to be my husband. I haven't decided which yet, but I'm going to be making somebody a very, very happy man today. Now let's be realistic,' she said, looking serious, 'only one of you will hit the jackpot . . .' She pointed at herself. '. . . but I want you to know that by making it this far you're all champions to me.'

She put down her megaphone, and gracefully hopped up onto the float, where she sat high above us on a gilded throne. Pulled by a tractor, we joined the cavalcade, every man smiling and waving at the crowds as if his life depended on it, each of us hoping with all his heart that her gaze would settle on him, that he would be the one to hold her hand again, and stroke her hair, and laugh at her jokes, and surprise her with flowers. As one, we ached to gaze into those incredible eyes, and kiss those soft, soft lips, and tell her over and over again how much we loved her.

PROMISE II

My wife told me she was leaving. 'But you can't,' I said. 'Don't you remember our vows? You promised to love me forever.'

'Vows?' she said. 'Promises?' With a hollow laugh, she asked me what century I thought I was living in.

SOMETHING

A few years into our marriage, my wife told me there was something she had always wanted to try. I asked her what it was, and she told me straight out. I had no idea what to say. 'Don't look at me like that,' she said. 'Everyone's at least a little bit kinky. I bet there's something *you* really like.' She looked at me through narrowed eyes. 'Well?'

Stammering, I told her I had always rather enjoyed it when she had gently nibbled my ears.

'So, there you are,' she snapped. 'You're in no position to judge.' I supposed she was right. It would have been hypocritical to refuse to cooperate, and I was left with no choice but to prepare the apparatus, hold my breath and brace myself.

TIME

Sunset told me she was leaving, and I couldn't hold back the tears. 'I don't know why you're crying,' she said. 'We've only been married a few weeks—that's no time at all.' She explained that she had been married to her last husband for three whole years, and when she had left him he had taken it like a man. 'There was certainly none of *this* business,' she said, pointing at my wet, contorted face.

Aqua told me she had started having misgivings about our vows. '*Love* is O.K., I suppose,' she said. 'It's quite weddingy, so it fits in. I'm not really sure what *honour* means, but I'll let it pass. I can't quite get my head around *obey*, though. It just doesn't seem right.'

The vicar asked her to hurry up, because the congregation was starting to get fidgety. 'I think I'm going to have to say . . .' She bit her lip and clicked her tongue. '. . . no. That's my final answer: a definite *no*. And if he's the kind of person who would expect me to say something like that, then I think I should marry somebody else.'

We had already paid for the reception, so it went ahead as planned. Aqua looked lovely in her dress, and spent the evening congratulating herself on her lucky escape, and dancing with handsome single men, every one of whom assured her that he would never ask her to obey him.

DRESS II

I agreed to go clothes shopping with my girl-friend. She went into the changing room, and to my surprise came out a while later wearing a wedding dress. I couldn't believe how beautiful she looked. 'So,' she said, 'what do you think?'

I had wanted to marry her for ages, but had never found the courage to ask. Swept away, there was nothing I could do but smile and say, 'Yes. Of course I'll marry you.'

She pulled a face. 'Oh God,' she said. 'I might have known something like this would happen.' She told me she was trying it on for a friend who was the same size as her. 'What makes you think I'd want *you* as a husband?'

I couldn't think of anything.

When I told my wife I was leaving, she was crushed. I didn't like to see her so unhappy, and I encouraged her to look on the bright side. 'Just think of all the material it'll give you for your songwriting,' I said.

'What songwriting?' she sobbed. 'I don't even play an instrument.'

'Well, you should start, especially now you've got all this inspiration.'

I convinced her to give it a try. She bought a piano, and before long she had composed a ballad called 'When You Left (My World Came Crashing Down)'. Unfortunately, it wasn't very good, and I had to tell her so; it wouldn't have been fair to let her think she was doing well. Disconsolate, she vowed never to play again.

Determined to be a good ex-husband, I helped her find a buyer for the abandoned instrument. 'What about sculpture?' I suggested. 'You could pour your pain into that instead.' She had a good try at it, but again I had to tell her that the result left an awful lot to be desired. She gave that up, too, and I did what I could to help her get a fair price for her chisels. I'll start her on oil painting next, but I'm not holding out much hope. With all that hurt eating away at her I'd have expected her to have created great work of some kind by now, but it's just not happening. I'm even starting to wonder whether she's really as upset as she says she is.

FEAR

My fiancée suggested we get married while strapped together and falling ten thousand feet from an aeroplane. I wasn't nearly as interested as she was in that kind of thing, and suggested we have a more conventional ceremony. She dismissed my misgivings. 'Feel the fear,' she said, 'and do it anyway. That's my motto.' Not wishing to appear unmanly, I went along with her plan, and I have to admit that in the event it was a lot of fun exchanging vows in mid-air while a vicar plummeted alongside us.

Unfortunately, our parachute has failed to open, and our marriage is looking likely to prove shortlived. She's screaming in terror, and I'm wondering whether this would be a good moment to remind her that it had been her idea.

BLUE

Without giving her the slightest warning, I told my wife I was leaving.

'O.K.,' she said. 'Bye, then.'

In case she had misunderstood, I explained that I wouldn't be coming back.

She shrugged. 'Fine,' she said. 'If that's your decision.'

'Are you going to be O.K.?' I asked.

'Why wouldn't I be O.K.?'

I had expected there to be at least a little scene after such monumental news from out of the blue, and a part of me was disappointed that she was taking things so calmly. I had even rehearsed a speech in which I told her not to cry, and assured her that she would, in time, find love with somebody else. Instead of delivering it, I just walked away. Halfway down the garden path I realised I'd forgotten to pack my favourite mug, so I crept back inside.

I was relieved to find her curled in a ball on the sofa, hugging a framed wedding photograph, loudly repeating my name, and bawling like a toddler who's left their bear on the train.

Promise III

As I held her in my arms on our wedding night, Anemone said, 'You remember all that stuff we said earlier, about staying together forever, and never doing it with anyone else?' I nodded. 'We're not going to take that *too* seriously, are we?'

REACH

My fiancée died. With tears in their eyes, her mother and father told me there had been a tradition in their ancestral village for the bereaved man to marry the deceased's younger sister. Though they understood that we were all leading modern lives, they implored us to respect this ancient code.

I was far too heartbroken to consider a new romance, and to complicate things further her sister and I had never found any common ground. We both knew how much it would mean to her parents, though, and after a private talk we agreed to play along for a while. Inevitably, we got on each other's nerves—she with her free-spirited ways and eccentric fashion sense, and me with my stubbornly conventional lifestyle and wardrobe.

Gradually, we realised we had more in common than we'd thought, and even began to learn from one another—me to loosen up, and she to take a little more responsibility for herself. Together we were able to find the strength we needed to get through this difficult time, and at last we reached a point where we were able to laugh again. With this new familiarity came real fondness, and though we both tried to run from these emotions, they were just too strong. One day, in a scenic location, we found ourselves locked in a romantic embrace.

It's worked out well: her parents are happy; we're now properly engaged rather than just pretending; and we've even sold our story to Hollywood. A bittersweet culture clash romcom, *Marrying May Wong,* is about to open at over three thousand locations, before being rolled out across forty-two international territories. Early research suggests it has a wide demographic reach, considerable prerelease awareness and a good chance of a strong opening weekend.

CHURCH II

My fiancée had never been even slightly religious, but all the talk of God during our marriage ceremony got her thinking, and she started to believe. As a result, our wedding night wasn't quite what I had hoped it would be. 'There's no way I'm taking all my clothes off with *Him* watching,' she said.

BRAVE

My wife gave me a big hug, and told me I was going to have to be very brave. 'I'm really sorry,' she said, 'but I just don't think I can carry on being married to you.'

I couldn't understand why she would walk out on everything we had. 'Is there somebody else?' I asked.

'No,' she said, 'there isn't. But I would really, *really* like there to be.'

Commitment

My bride had invited a number of her exes to our wedding, and as she walked down the aisle I could see she was flashing them coquettish smiles, waving to them, and winking. I started to feel a little concerned that she wasn't ready to move on to a new level of commitment, but I needn't have worried. When she reached the altar she asked the vicar to wait for a moment while she delivered a short speech. 'There are several men in here with whom I have had sexual encounters,' she said, 'but I want you all to know that I'm going to be taking my marriage very seriously. Though there may be some residual attraction between us, it's very important for you to understand that I will never act on it.'

It was so sweet of her to give me this reassurance, but as I looked out at the faces of the men she had known I had a feeling that not all of them were as convinced as I was by her declaration.

In Common

Midnight told me she was calling off our engagement, and I did what I could to talk her out of it. 'But we have so much in common,' I spluttered. 'We both like spring meadows and autumn leaves; we read the same poets and admire the same artists and musicians. And what about Spaniels?' I cried in desperation. 'We both love Spaniels, don't we?'

'That's the trouble,' she said. 'I think they're O.K., but I'm not crazy about them. It's the same with the other stuff—there's nothing wrong with any of it, but it's all more your thing than mine.'

TEST

I opened my front door to find my girlfriend standing there. I was delighted to see her, and invited her in for a coffee. As the kettle boiled, she came straight out with the reason for her visit: she had come to tell me she was pregnant. I was stunned, but overjoyed.

'Don't you worry,' I said, throwing my arms around her and holding her tight. 'I'll be here for you and the baby. In fact, why don't we get married?' I'd been thinking about asking her for ages, but the right moment had never arisen. Now the time couldn't have seemed more perfect. 'We'll be a family.'

She started laughing. 'That's so funny,' she said. 'You're the fourth one to use those exact words, and I've still got . . .' she pulled a list from her pocket, and counted, '. . . eight to go.' She pinched my cheeks. 'You're all so sweet,' she said, then she stopped laughing, and lowered her eyes. 'I'll say to you what I said to the others—just take the test, and if it's yours I'll think about it.'

NEST

When I told my fiancée I was cancelling the wedding, I was quick to alert her to the upside of the situation. 'Just think of all the money you'll save by not being with me,' I said. 'With all those nights in alone in front of the television, you'll be able to build up quite the nest egg. All you'll be wearing is pyjamas, and as long as you stick to supermarket brand ice cream, rather than the fancy stuff, you'll have a decent lump sum in no time at all.'

WORST

My wife told me that she and her friends had voted me the worst at sex out of all their husbands. 'But how could they know?' I asked.

'I told them about that thing you do with your fingers,' she said. 'That thing you think I really like. They couldn't stop laughing; they thought it was hilarious.'

The time came for me to tell my fiancée I had found somebody new, and that I was breaking things off with her. 'I can't be engaged to you and going out with her at the same time,' I explained. 'It doesn't feel right.'

Frantic, she started to list her own qualities in the hope that I would realise what I was throwing away and come to my senses. It didn't work, though. I was adamant that I liked the other girl more, and I wouldn't back down. At last, she accepted that it was over. 'I suppose she's really beautiful, and I just can't compete,' she sobbed.

'Well, that's the funny thing,' I replied. 'Technically, you're a lot better-looking than she is, but I still like her more. It's a *je ne sais quoi* thing, I suppose.'

She insisted I take her to have a look at the new girl. We hid in some bushes near her house, and watched her through binoculars. 'Wow,' said my ex-fiancée. 'Are you serious? You're leaving *me* for *her*?'

'I know,' I said. 'It's weird.'

On our first anniversary I held Maranatha's hand, looked into her eyes and told her that even though I wouldn't have thought it possible I loved her even more deeply than I had on our wedding day.

'It's funny,' she said. 'I've gone *completely* the other way. Come to think of it, I'm amazed I've stayed as long as I have. There's *no way* I'm going to be here next year.'

Every girl I had ever cared about had gone away, and I knew Alanta would, too. From the moment we met I braced myself for her departure, but as I waited for the axe to fall, my love for her grew deeper and deeper. It got to the point where I couldn't imagine life without her. Gathering all my courage, but expecting the worst, I asked her to marry me.

I couldn't believe it when she said yes.

As we stood before the altar, she looked at me with eyes that seemed to be overflowing with happiness, but deep down I knew she would make a run for it at the last minute. The time came for the vows, and she said them all the way through. She let me put the ring on her finger, and when she kissed me a tear came to her eye. As our lips parted, she softly whispered, *I love you*. It was strange. It was almost as if she really meant it.

ANDROIDS

My fiancée had always been keen on science fiction, and when she suggested we dress as androids on our wedding day I knew how happy it would make her, so I was glad to go along with it. I found myself waiting nervously at the altar in my Cyberman costume, and when I saw her coming down the aisle in her custom-made C3P0 outfit, my heart melted. Because of her helmet, I was unable to see the anger on her face. She stood beside me, and hissed, 'A Cyberman? Cybermen aren't androids, they're cyborgs. Jesus.' Her fury turned to dismay, and she began to sob. 'I can't believe you would do this to me on my wedding day.' Then there was a flash and a bang and the smell of electrical burning.

When they cut her lifeless body from her casing, the doctors said that her tears must have dripped into the circuit board and triggered a massive power surge. At the inquest they concluded that even an elephant wouldn't have survived such a shock. The coroner, also a fan of the genre, expressed disbelief that I could have made such an error, and told me that I must blame myself.

As our wedding day approached, my fiancée gently suggested that I get some counselling for my body image issues. 'But, darling,' I chuckled, 'I don't have any body image issues.'

'That's the problem,' she said. 'Just look at yourself. You'd better get some—and fast.'

I was delighted to find a foreign girlfriend, and even more delighted when she agreed to marry me. 'It'll be such a happy day,' I said.

'Happy?' she said, looking aghast. 'I don't think you understand.' In her endearing accent, she explained that in her culture, weddings were not times of celebration; they were desolate affairs that marked the end of youth and freedom. She was determined to adhere to her country's traditions, so a few months later I found myself helplessly looking on as she wept real tears for the girl she had once been, while trampling a bunch of flowers underfoot, symbolising the exit of even the slightest possibility of romance from her life. Her relatives, unable by custom to console her, glared at me and shook their heads, as if wondering how I could have done this to such a sweet girl.

LEAGUE

My fiancée gazed into my eyes. 'I never thought I would get to marry someone as handsome as you,' she said.

This got me thinking. 'I am a bit out of your league, aren't I?'

She began to look afraid. 'But you will still marry me?'

'Leave it with me,' I said. 'I'll get back to you in a day or two.'

News II

After a lot of soul searching, I reached the con-
clusion that I was no longer in love with my
fiancée, and the only fair thing for both of us
would be for me to call off the wedding.
Moments later, news came through that she
had lost her hands in an industrial accident. I
rushed to the hospital, and as she lay weeping
at the sight of her bandaged stumps it didn't
seem like the right time to tell her how I felt. I
chose not to raise the subject, and instead
found myself whispering empty words of love
and reassuring her that we would get through
this difficulty together.

She was determined to stick to our planned
wedding date; she told me it would be a part
of her recovery process. The closer it got, the

harder it became for me to find the right moment to initiate the Big Conversation. Finally, the day arrived, and as I stood at the altar and saw her father proudly leading her down the aisle, I realised I couldn't leave it any longer.

She looked up at me, her eyes ablaze with joy, as the vicar asked me if I was ready to take her as my wife. I surprised myself by telling him I was, and I even found myself saying my vows with real feeling. Somewhere along the line, without realising it, I had fallen back in love with her. It ended up being just like any normal wedding—apart from her ring, which was more like a bangle.